HILLTOP ELEMENTARY SCHOOL

JOE LOUIS, MY CHAMPION

BY William Miller • ILLUSTRATED BY Rodney S. Pate

Lee & Low Books Inc. • New York

LEE & LOW BOOKS Inc., 95 Madison Avenue, New York, NY 10016
leeandlow.com

Manufactured in China

Book design by Christy Hale
Book production by The Kids at Our House

The text is set in Cochin
The illustrations are rendered in oil paint on canvas paper

10 9 8 7 6 5 4 3 2 1
First Edition

Library of Congress Cataloging-in-Publication Data
Miller, William.
Joe Louis, my champion / by William Miller ; illustrated by Rodney S. Pate.— 1st ed.
p. cm.
Summary: After listening to the radio broadcast of the heavyweight championship
boxing fight of his hero, Joe Louis, a young African American boy realizes that he
can emulate the boxer's persistence and strive to become whatever he wants to be.
ISBN 1-58430-161-9
[1. Persistence—Fiction. 2. Heroes—Fiction. 3. Prejudices—Fiction.
4. Louis, Joe 1914—Fiction 5. Boxers (Sports)—Fiction.
6. African Americans—Fiction.] I. Pate, Rodney S., ill. II. Title.
PZ7.M63915Jo 2004
[E]—dc21   2003008999

For Julian Bartley,
father, boxer, friend
—W.M.

To M. Davey, B. Griffin
and J. Francis
—R.S.P.

Everybody at school was talking about the big fight.
In a month Joe Louis was boxing James Braddock for the
heavyweight championship of the world. All the kids thought
Big Joe was going to win, and so did I.

I loved Joe Louis so much, I tore a picture of him out of a
magazine and carried it in my back pocket. I was just a little
guy and not very good at sports, but Big Joe was my hero.
I wanted to be a boxer just like him.

When the school bell rang, I ran out the door with
my best friend, Ernie Block. Ernie was the biggest
kid in my class. He gave me boxing lessons, and
I helped him with his schoolwork.

"Ready for your lesson, Sammy?" Ernie asked, stopping under a cypress tree and putting his palms up for me to punch.

I dropped my books and crouched into a boxer's stance.

"Stick and move, stick and move," said Ernie. "That's it—left cross, right hook."

I swung as hard as I could but missed Ernie's hand. I punched again and again, but soon my arms got tired.

"You're getting there," Ernie said. "Don't give up."

"Thanks," I said, but I was discouraged. I was beginning to think I'd never learn how to box.

When I got home, Papa was sitting in his favorite rocking chair, taking a rest from his farm work. Mama was sweeping the porch like she always did each afternoon.

"Why are you looking so blue, Sammy?" asked Papa.

"I'll never be a famous boxer like Joe Louis," I blurted out. "My arms are too short, and I'm not fast enough. I wish I were big and strong like Ernie."

"There's only one Joe Louis," Papa said. "But I suspect Joe gets thirsty just like everybody else. Let's walk down to Mister Jake's and get us a cold drink."

Papa put his arm around my shoulder, and together we walked down the dusty road.

Mister Jake's country store was my favorite place. Pictures of Joe Louis and news stories about his boxing matches were on every wall. And there on the table was Mister Jake's radio—the only one in the valley. It was made of dark wood and had a bright shiny dial.

"Mister Jake, Sammy loves Joe Louis, just like the rest of us," Papa explained. "But maybe there's something about Joe he doesn't know."

Mister Jake laughed his big belly laugh and popped his suspenders. Then he began saying how Joe Louis had been a farm boy just like me, but with plenty of hard work and training, he had fought his way to the top of the boxing world, one ring at a time.

"Joe's had to fight something else too," said Mister Jake. "Sammy, do you know what prejudice is?"

"Sure, Mister Jake," I said. "It's when some people don't think other people are as good as them."

"You're right, Sammy," said Mister Jake. "And that's why Joe Louis means more to us than boxing. Joe's shown the world a colored person is as good as anyone. He can be the best at anything he wants to be."

I tried to pay attention to what Mister Jake was saying, but I couldn't keep my mind off his big radio. Everyone for miles around would be listening to the boxing match on that radio next month. Papa promised we'd be here with everybody else, listening from the first bell to the last.

"There's no quit in Joe Louis," Papa said. "Win or lose, he'll still be a great boxer."

"For sure," said Mister Jake. "So tell me, Sammy, do you think Joe Louis is going to win the fight against James Braddock?"

I looked up at all the pictures of Joe Louis on the wall. "Big Joe's going to put him down hard," I said. "He's going to be heavyweight champion of the world!"

"Now that's what I wanted to hear," Mister Jake said as he popped his suspenders again.

When the night of the big fight finally arrived, we got to Mister Jake's store early and took seats right beside the radio. I was so excited I could hardly sit still. Folks who came later had to stand and listen. The porch and yard were filled with people—men, women, children, and even babies sleeping in their mamas' arms. Everyone was anxious for the fight to begin.

I saw Ernie across the room. We waved to each other, and I could tell by the grin on his face that he was just as excited as I was.

"Remember, Sammy," Papa whispered in my ear. "Joe Louis is a champ, no matter who wins the match. He's lost fights before, but he always does his best. That's why he's a great man."

"There's no quit in Big Joe!" I said, and Papa laughed.

Mister Jake turned up the radio, and everything went quiet.

B-O-O-O-N-G! rang the bell for the first round to begin.

The radio announcer told us everything that was happening. In the first round, both boxers bobbed and weaved. Braddock dodged Joe Louis's punches but then surprised everyone when he caught Joe with a hard right. Big Joe hit the mat and didn't get up.

Everybody groaned, and then the room grew silent.

I was worried. Could the fight be over already? Could Joe Louis really lose?

Slowly Big Joe pulled himself up, and in a moment he was standing. He didn't go for a knockout punch but started hitting Braddock with combinations—left hooks and right uppercuts—wearing him down more and more with each round.

Folks started to clap, then stomp their feet. Big Joe was coming back!

By the eighth round Braddock could barely stand. Everyone around me was shouting, but I didn't hear them. I was thinking about Joe Louis toe-to-toe with Braddock. Big Joe was tired, almost ready to quit, but he refused to go down. His feet started moving again, gloves raised.

"You can do it, Joe," I whispered. "You're the greatest boxer in the world!"

Big Joe threw one more right, and Braddock dropped to the mat. Then the long count began.

"One . . . two . . . three . . . four . . . five . . . six . . . seven . . . eight . . . nine . . . ten!"

"Hurray!" "Yea!" The crowd exploded into wild cheers and shouts.

"Joe Louis is the heavyweight champion of the world!" I cried, and Papa gave me a hug. We were all champions now—every one of us who believed in Joe Louis.

The next day I went to visit Ernie. He was waiting for me under a shade tree.

"That was some fight," Ernie said. "I almost thought Joe Louis was going down, but he stayed in there."

"He sure did," I said, and put up my fists. "I'm going to be a great boxer someday, just like Big Joe!"

Ernie laughed and held up his palms. I swung and swung while Ernie told me to "stick and move." I kept thinking about the last punch Joe Louis threw—the one that took down Braddock. I swung with my right fist so hard, I missed Ernie's hand and fell in the dirt. I felt foolish and ashamed.

"Hey, Sammy," said Ernie, helping me up. "So what if you're never a good boxer."

"What do you mean?" I asked, brushing the dirt from my clothes, trying hard not to cry.

"You're really smart," Ernie said. "You get good grades in school. You don't have to be good at boxing too."

I heard what Ernie was saying, but I still wanted to be a boxer more than anything. Ernie just didn't understand.

I ran away with tears in my eyes.

I lay by the creek for the longest time, until it started
to get dark. I took the picture of Big Joe from my pocket
and looked at it. I was so proud of him. Joe Louis was the
heavyweight champion of the world, and I wanted to be
just like him.

Finally I walked back to the farm. Papa was waiting for me on the porch. He caught me by the arm and asked me what was wrong. He looked more worried than angry.

"I'll never be a boxer like Joe Louis," I said sadly. "I keep trying to throw good punches, but I can't. I'll never be a champ."

"Sammy, remember the day we went to Mister Jake's a few weeks ago?" Papa asked. "He told you some things about Big Joe you didn't know."

I wasn't sure what Papa meant. But then I remembered. "Mister Jake said Joe Louis had to work hard to be the best boxer in the world, and if he could do it, colored folks could be the best at anything they want to be."

"That's right, Sammy," Papa said. "You can be a champion at anything you want."

I walked out into the field. The sun was dark red, just about to set. As I looked at the hills far off in the distance, I thought about the towns and cities that lay beyond—places I might go one day.

Maybe I'd never be a boxer, but I could be good at something else. I saw myself in front of a judge, fighting the way lawyers do for poor people. I saw myself wearing a doctor's long, white coat, helping sick people. I saw myself in front of a blackboard, teaching kids in school.

As the sun went down behind the hills, I looked at my picture of Joe Louis. No matter where I went, no matter what I became, that picture would remind me I could be the best. Joe Louis had taught me that. He was my hero. He was *my* champion!

Afterword

JOE LOUIS is widely regarded as the finest heavyweight champion in the history of boxing. He was also the first African American to achieve hero status for all Americans—an honor previously reserved only for whites.

The "Brown Bomber," as Louis came to be known, was a role model for everyone, but he was especially inspirational to African Americans. During a time when African Americans were subject to segregation and discrimination in their daily lives, Joe Louis was a symbol of achievement and power. His public prominence and popularity empowered African Americans at a time when they felt powerless.

Joseph Louis Barrow was born in Alabama in 1914. After his family moved to Detroit in the mid-1920s, he became fascinated with boxing. He began training at age seventeen and soon after shortened his name to Joe Louis. He won 50 out of 54 amateur bouts and turned professional in 1934. As a pro, Louis won his first 27 fights, but in his 28th fight he met defeat by former heavyweight champion Max Schmeling of Germany. Louis rebounded to win his next seven bouts, and on June 22, 1937, he captured the heavyweight crown with an eighth-round knockout of the reigning champion, James J. Braddock. Louis held the heavyweight title for twelve years, longer than any other fighter. He still holds this record today.

Boxing in the 1930s through the 1950s was a popular sport enjoyed by every segment of society, and people of all ages and backgrounds would gather around their radios to listen when Joe Louis defended his title. His career was based on hard work and determination, and he was admired for his dignity, sportsmanship, and good humor. Upon Louis's death in 1981 at the age of sixty-six, Jersey Joe Walcott, his opponent in two title fights, said, "He was a great fighter, and a great champion in and out of the ring. He was symbolic to all people, young and old, black and white. . . . We lost one of the great Americans."